A Tall Story Book

An Adventure for Teddy Bear

A Tall Story Book

An Adventure for Teddy Bear

Illustrated by Douglas Hall

GALLERY BOOKS
An Imprint of W. H. Smith Publishers Inc.
112 Madison Avenue
New York City 10016

Teddy was trying out
his new boat.
But suddenly a breeze
blew the boat out
into the river, and Teddy
lost his paddle.
He tried to reach it,
but it quickly floated away.
"Help!" he cried,
but nobody could hear him.

Teddy found it difficult
to stay in the boat as the
river tumbled down to the sea.
He shouted to the sheep
and the lamb, on the bank.

"Can you help? I can't steer without a paddle."

"No-o, but we would if we could," said the sheep.

"Baa, we would if we could," said the lamb.

The river turned a sharp bend and on the other bank Teddy saw a cow and a calf.

"Help! Can you help?" shouted Teddy.

"Noo-oo," said the cow, "but we would if we could."

"Moo-oo," said the calf, "I wish we could."

Bouncing over rocks and swirling water, Teddy's boat reached the sea. Teddy saw a horse near the shore.

"Quick, quick," Teddy cried, "I've lost my paddle. Can you help me?"

"Neigh, neigh," answered the horse. "I cannot reach you – if only I could."

"HELP!" cried Teddy,
as a big curling wave
flung him head over heels
into the tossing sea.
"Good thing I learned to
swim yesterday," thought
Teddy. Then suddenly he
found himself sitting on
a big gray-blue animal.

"Hello Teddy," he said. "I'm Doddle the Dolphin. I heard you calling for help my young wet friend. I'll soon have you safe, so sit back and enjoy the ride home."

Teddy has visited Doddle many times since that

exciting ride, and when the wind and tide are just right, Teddy and Doddle play "rescue" games all day long, until it's time to go to bed.

This edition published by

GALLERY BOOKS
An Imprint of W. H. Smith Publishers Inc.
112 Madison Avenue
New York City 10016

Prepared by
Deans International Publishing
52–54 Southwark Street, London SE1 1UA
A division of The Hamlyn Publishing Group Limited
London · New York · Sydney · Toronto

ISBN 0-8317-0066-1

Printed in Great Britain